JOAN VEGAS

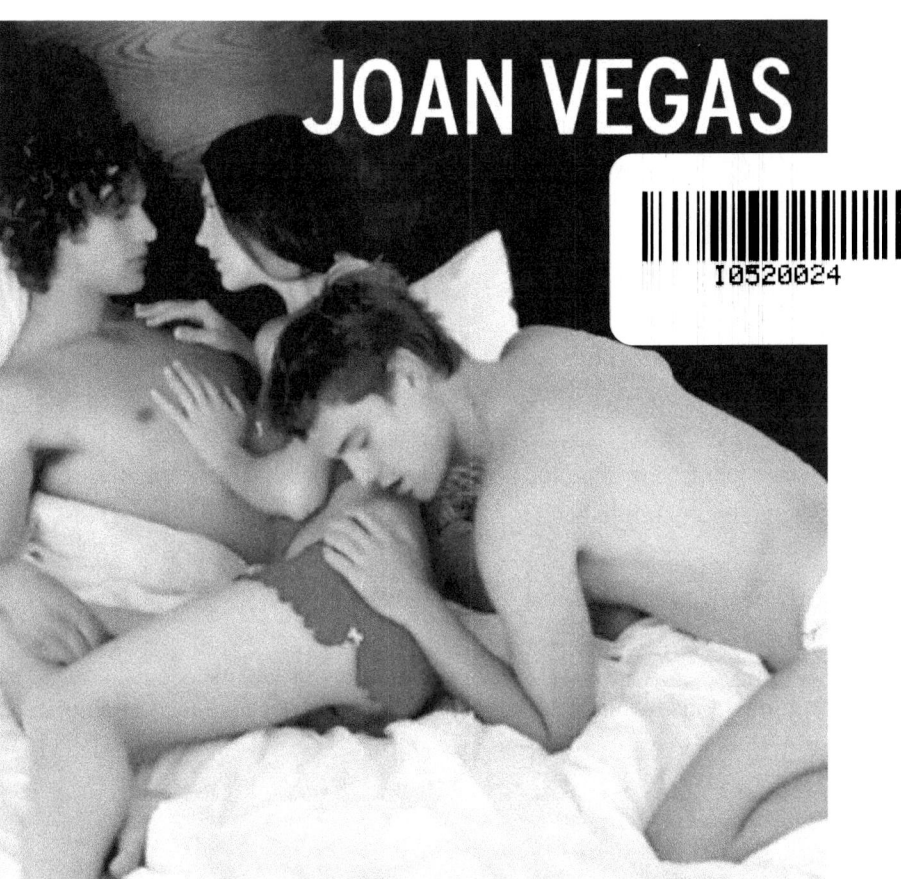

THE MORE, THE MERRIER

FOUR WOMEN REPORT ON HAVING TWO (OR MORE) HUSBANDS

THREESOME-AWESOME SEX

WARNING

This book contains sexually explicit scenes and adult language. It may be considered offensive to some readers. This book is for sale to adults ONLY.

* * * * * * * * * * * * * * * * * * * *

Please store your files wisely where they cannot be accessed by underage readers.

Please feel free to send me an email. Just know that these emails are filtered by my publisher. Good news is always welcome.

Joan Vegas - **joan_vegas@awesomeauthors.org**

You might also want to check my blog for updates and interesting info.
http://joan-vegas.awesomeauthors.org/

About the Publisher

4Fun Publishing, a member of **BLVNP Incorporated**, 340 S. Lemon #6200, Walnut CA 91789, info@blvnp.com / legal@blvnp.com
NOTE: Due to the highly emotional reaction of some people to works of erotic fiction, any email sent to the above address that contains foul language or religious references is automatically deleted by our anti-spam software and will not be seen. All other communications are welcome.

DISCLAIMER

Please don't be stupid and kill yourself. This book is a work of FICTION. Do not try any new sexual practice that you find in this book. It is fiction and not to be confused with reality. Neither the author nor the publisher or its associates assume any responsibility for any loss, injury, death or legal consequences resulting from acting on the contents in this book. Every character in this book is over 18 years of age. The author's opinions are not to be construed as the opinions of the publisher. The material in this book is for entertainment purposes ONLY. Enjoy.

The More, The Merrier

Four Women Report On Having
Two (or more) Husbands

Threesome-Awesome Sex

By: Joan Vegas

ISBN: 978-1-62761-686-7

The Joy of Having
A Second 'Hubby'

Joe and I had been married for a fairly short time when we met Marv. We had bought an old house and neither Joe nor I knew much about fixing up the place.

Home Depot helped by giving lessons on different things but we constantly ran into problems with things we hadn't had experience with.

Luckily Marv, a friend of Joe's from work, offered to help. He is older, maybe 30, and a nice guy. Joe was 24 at the time, and I was 22. Marv was in a troubled marriage, and would sometime stay at our house on weekends. We all got along fine.

I would tease and flirt with him, not thinking anything of it. After all, we were just friends. One night he showed up devastated, saying his wife had left him. He was crying. She had taken their kids and moved back to Missouri with some guy she had met.

He was so broken up that although Joe tried to comfort him, it was clumsy. I took him and held him, letting him cry. It was heartbreaking to hear his wracking sobs and his body shaking with grief.

At the time our little one bedroom home had very few furnishings. In the living room we just had a TV and four frameless futons to sit on. When Marv arrived that night we were already in bed. Hearing the doorbell ring, Joe and I just put our robes on to see who it was. Mine was just a short robe, and (like Joe) I had nothing on underneath as we answered the door.

I was sitting on one of our futons in our living room, leaning against the wall when I called Marv over to me so I could console him. He sat down next to me. I was holding him tight, patting his back, cuddling him against me, and saying dumb things to him. I'm not sure when it happened, but one moment he was sobbing on my shoulder, then the next he was kissing me. I was too shocked to react.

I looked up at Joe only to find that he was smiling and mouthing the words "It's OK… comfort him."

Soon Marv's head was in my lap with his body and legs stretched out on the futon. That's when I noticed the top two buttons on my robe had come undone, and my robe was gaping open. I noticed that Marv was looking at my bare boobs, but my arms were trapped under him so I couldn't move to cover myself.

As I continued to cradle Marv in my arms, I felt him pull himself up to give me another kiss. As he did that he placed one of his hands on my nearest breast and began to fondle it. I started to pull away when I heard Joe say, "Hon, let him play. That will help him relax and forget his troubles." I was a bit bewildered at my husband's words, but I stopped pulling away and let Marv play with my breasts. Soon he was kissing one while playing with my other one… and I was just letting him. When I looked over at my husband I found that he was just grinning… obviously not unhappy about what Marv was doing with me… his wife.

Marv had stopped crying and was clearly enjoying himself in my arms as he alternately sucked my breasts. I knew my husband had sat down on one of the other futons and was watching. While still cradling Marv in my arms, boobs exposed to his play, I again looked over at my husband. He whispered, "He needs this, Hon. Go ahead."

I wasn't quite sure what "Go ahead" meant. By then, my back had slipped away from the wall and my head had settled back on one of the other futons. As Marv continued to feast on my boobs I began to feel at ease with my mother-like role of letting him suckle me while I comforted him. Besides, it felt good to feel the hands and mouth of another man playing on my body.

I saw my husband move over by my feet. My lower body was lying flat with Marv's head and shoulder at about my waist level.

I felt my husband undo the one remaining button on the lower portion of my short robe. Then he nudged my legs apart. He crawled between my legs and planted his face against my crotch.

With Marv still gently sucking one of my breasts, I felt Joe's tongue begin to flutter over my clit. What a sensation… two men playing with different parts of my body. I was getting turned-on.

Then I felt my husband's tongue dip inside my pussy. I love it when he does that… and it felt especially good that night, in that setting, with Marv's mouth sucking my nipple. I felt my body begin to involuntarily twist and buck a bit against my husband's face. I think I also hugged Marv more tightly against my chest… unintentionally encouraging him to suck harder on me. With his hand he cupped my other breast before squeezing that nipple.

The combination of those sensations sent me over the top. I squirmed and let out a throaty groan as I felt an unexpected but delightful orgasm pass through my body.

As I gradually recovered from that orgasm I realized that Marv had pulled away and was removing his clothes. Joe had moved away from my crotch, but my legs were still spread. I was confused, and I guess that's when Marv made his move. As I continued to lay back on the futon Marv positioned himself above me, letting his legs fall between my spread legs. I realized he was about to fuck me.

I quickly looked at Joe. He again had a smile on his face and was licking his lips as Marv moved above me. I began to realize what my husband meant earlier when he said, "He needs this, Hon. Go ahead." My husband was giving me permission to let Marv fuck me!

Although I had started to resist Marv's moves atop me, I just gave up and relaxed. Marv wedged himself between my legs, and I felt his dick probing my pussy. I couldn't believe that my Joe was letting this happen. I felt the head of Marv's dick slip into me. I gasped as Marv began to fuck me, too shocked to resist. It was starting to feel really good, and I felt my body responding to him.

I am sure my face flushed with a combination of shame, disbelief and disorientation as my body began to move underneath Marv. In no time my arms were wrapped tightly around his neck. It felt good to have a new and different cock playing within me. He grunted, thrusting himself into me, and I felt his hot seed as he ejaculated inside my pussy. He lay on top of me for a while, and I felt his cock pulse as he continued to spurt within me.

When Marv realized what he had done he jumped up saying, 'I'm sorry, Maria. I'm sorry. I don't know what came over me." He pulled his clothes on and dashed from the house.

I lay there dazed, trying to figure out what had just happened. I saw Joe move over by me. I was still in shock, and my body was still tingeing from my sexual encounter with Marv. Although I had enjoyed an orgasm before Marv entered me, by then my body was again in need of release.

I felt Joe's tongue probe my pussy, and I said, "You can't do that. Marv just came inside me." But Joe's tongue kept probing my pussy, and it felt so good I just lay there as my husband licked Marv's cum out of me.

I looked down and saw some of Marv's cum on Joe's tongue. He was scooping it out of my pussy. I had a very explosive orgasm while Joe ate me. Then I came once more when Joe then fucked me like a deranged animal.

Joe and I managed to make our way back to bed. Once there, we cuddled and repeatedly whispered our love for each other, to each other. As Joe held me, he confessed that over the previous several weeks, he and Marv had talked about how I had been flirting with Marv… and he with me.

I quickly let Joe know that I had always considered it innocent flirting and had never expected to be intimate with Marv. Joe hugged me, smiled and said, "I know babe. But it got me to thinking that it would be cool to see my best friend give special pleasure to my loving wife." He went on to tell me that he encouraged Marv to keep flirting with me… and, if the situation ever allowed it, he should feel free to screw me.

Hearing that, I pulled back and said, "You really told him that?" He shook his head affirmatively and said, "And I am glad I did!"

I was quiet for a while. Then I hugged my hubby and said, "I guess I am glad you did too." I gave him a passionate kiss and admitted to him that it had felt good to have another man's cock within me, throbbing and ejaculating within me. "I sure am glad I am on the pill though," I told him.

By then Joe was hard again and he entered me. "It was really cool to watch Marv enter you, pump you, and then unload inside you," he said. As Joe gently pumped inside me he went on, "And, I want to watch Marv do that to you again." I didn't reply. Soon we both had enjoyable climaxes and fell asleep.

The next morning, a Saturday, Joe and I discussed what we had done the night before, talked about our friendship with Marv, and considered Marv's dilemma now that his wife and kids were gone.

I had always enjoyed the sex play that Joe and I shared, and I had already admitted to him that I enjoyed the sex I had with three different guys I dated before meeting him. So, it was easy for me to admit I had enjoyed the sex with Marv the night before. After admitting that, I asked if he was serious about wanting to watch Marv have sex with me again. He quickly replied, "Yes again… and again… and again." I could only answer "Wow!"

By that point in our conversation, we had both had a couple cups of coffee but we hadn't had breakfast. As a matter of fact we were still in our robes. Joe said, "How about I call Marv and see if he wants to come over and have breakfast with us?" I just told him I would be fine with that.

He got on the phone and soon reached Marv. I could tell from listening to Joe's end of the conversation that Marv had apologized again for having had sex with me. I heard Joe say, "No need to apologize. Just come join us for breakfast."

I quickly showered, and it was not long before Marv showed up. Joe, with a big grin on his face, reached his hand out and shook Marv's hand. Then, to demonstrate that I was not unhappy with him, I wrapped my arms around him and gave him a big hug. Then I smiled at him as I said, "Marv, Joe and I have talked. We both enjoyed last night… especially me!"

I fixed breakfast for all of us. We chatted as I fixed the breakfast and as we ate it. "I'm glad you guys are not mad at me," Marv offered, "but I am still sorry I came so fast… I didn't give Maria an orgasm before I shot off."

By then we were done eating. I stood up, took Marv's hand and said, "Well there is still time to correct that."

As Marv stood up, I grabbed Joe's hand. "I want both of you… now," and led them back to our still rumpled bed.

Over the next two hours both guys took turns necking with me, and nibbled on my breasts as I played with their hard cocks. They gave me several orgasms before Marv finally drove his hard cock into my very moist pussy. That time he was determined to give me an orgasm while he was playing inside me. He did, and then he filled me with his cum again.

Then Joe slipped his hard cock into me… slowly… telling me he was enjoying the cum-lube that Marv had left in my love channel. We all talked as Joe told Marv and me how neat "sloppy seconds" felt. He too took me over the top before he unloaded inside me.

That day, between passion-filled sessions in bed, we decided Marv should give up his rental apartment (since his wife and kids were gone) and move in with us. In the past when he spent the night with us he had always slept on one of the futons. Joe told him that if he accepted our offer he would be sharing our king-size bed with us. I didn't say anything, but my husband's words made my pussy wet in anticipation of what that could mean.

The next day, with Joe's help, Marv moved in. That was the start of my effectively having two husbands. Of course Joe is my real husband and primary lover, but once we all go to bed together I get the unparalleled pleasure of have two attentive lovers. I loved the constant attention. We were all young and full of life. Sometimes the two of them would fuck me for hours at a time.

Typical of our shared playfulness, one night we were sitting around after dinner. There wasn't anything on TV that was interesting. I said, "Let's play strip poker," and they both immediately liked my idea. We got out the cards, and since I am a lousy cards player, I was soon sitting there nude. I gave them my little girl look, and said, "Well guys, I don't have anything else to bet. What do we do now?"

Marv rubbed his hands together, leering at me, and in his best impression of WC Fields' voice he said, "Well my little chickadee, we will come up with something. Deal the cards Joe." Marv won, and Joe had a better hand than mine. Marv smiled widely and scooted his chair back. He still had his pants and T-shirt on. Joe was down to his T-shirt and shorts.

Marv dropped his pants and said, "Come here 'little chickadee,' since you lost, you have to suck my cock." I covered my mouth with my hand and in mock horror. His dick was pressed tightly against his belly, begging for attention.

I said, "Oh my, such uncouth language." Joe laughed and said, "Come on, give him some head." Marv sat down on the chair, spreading his legs wide so I could get at his dick as my Joe looked on.

I knelt in front of Marv and hooked his cock with my index finger. I looked up at him, teasing him with my eyes. His breath was getting faster, watching my mouth that close to his dick. I licked my lips and spit in my hand, rubbing it on his cock slowly, jacking his shaft.

I asked, "Do you like this?" Then I leaned over and a long stream of my saliva covered his cock head. He was trying to fuck my hand, so I took the head of his cock in my mouth. His silky dick head tasted so good I was tempted to finish him off, but I was also feeling playful. I stood and said, "Well that's all for now!"

Marv said, "Oh please, you can't leave me this way." I giggled and said, "Yes I can." He leaped to his feet sputtering, "Come on. Please finish me off." His stiff cock slapped against his belly, and it looked so comical that I laughed. I said, "Catch me," and turned racing for the staircase. Marv let out a bellow, and I heard my husband say, "She's headed for the stairs."

I could hear Marv's bare feet slapping on the floor, and he was gaining on me when I tried to turn at the stairs. The throw rug slid, and I went to my knees. I was scrambling up the stairs on my hands and knees, laughing breathlessly when Marv yelled, "GOTCHA," and grabbed me. He was kneeling on the staircase behind me, and I could feel his body as it pressed against my bare ass.

He held me so I couldn't get away, and I felt him guiding his dick to my very wet pussy. He lurched forward and was instantly up to his balls inside me. Then he grabbed my hips and began to fuck me like crazy. I looked over to see that Joe was watching us while stroking his cock, almost at my eye level.

Marv was fucking me harder, and I could feel his balls slapping my clity. He grunted, and I felt his cock pulsing inside of me. He spasmodically thrust a few times. Then he held my pussy against him as I felt him come inside me. Marv let out a long satisfied breath, and I felt his cock losing its strength as he stroked it in and out. Then it fell lifelessly out of me.

At that point I was on the verge of a climax, and I whimpered with my need. Joe got behind me and replaced Marv. His stiff cock began hammering in and out of me, and I came very loudly.

After Joe came, the guys carried me upstairs and they both fucked me for a long time. Later when the guys were both lying on the bed with their soft cocks totally spent, I sat their looking at them… thinking, "Gee, if there was just one more guy."

During Marv's stay with us we did many things together. I never liked anal sex, so I had a rule against that during our sex play. Both guys honored my wishes. However one night they had me sandwiched between them as we lay in bed. Facing and necking with my hubby, I felt his hard cock slip between my vaginal lips. It felt good.

Marv was cuddled against my back and I could feel his hard cock against my butt. I felt Marv adjust himself so his cock was poking between my legs. I was about to remind him of my no-anal-sex rule when I felt him press more tightly against me… and then felt his cock join Joe's cock within my pussy. Wow! We had never done that before. My pussy felt extra full… and extra stimulated.

I saw a grin on Joe's face as he said, "Now that's a different feeling! Babe, do you like having both of us inside you at the same time?" It took me a moment to respond. When I did, I said, "Yes, I like the extra fullness, and the varying strokes the two are giving me in there."

It wasn't long before their cock-against-cock movements got them both so stimulated that both cocks swelled up at the same time. That expanded extra fullness within my pussy sent me over the top just as both of them emptied their nuts as they sprayed my insides. What a sensation!

As you might guess, that kind of double vaginal penetration became a regular part of our three-way sex play. I always loved being sandwiched between my two "husbands".

Marv had a tendency to wake in the morning before Joe and I did. I would often partially wake to feel Marv cuddled against my back, his fresh morning hard-on making its way between my legs and into my pussy. I would typically (almost involuntarily) press back to allow him more depth in my pussy. He usually was quiet and gentle as he stroked within me... until I felt him expand and give me my first filling of the day.

I would often twist over, give Marv a sleepy kiss, then twist back and go to sleep as he got out of bed. Marv got into a routine of making breakfast for all of us. The aroma of coffee and frying bacon usually woke Joe and me. Marv's example in regularly making breakfast motivated my Joe to, often, prepare our dinners. I liked that.

Marv lived with us for almost three years, before moving to another city to take a new job. Both Joe and I miss him. Since Marv left, to compensate for my no longer having two 'husbands', Joe has periodically brought a few of his friends home... treating me to MFM play. It's not quite the same as having two loving guys in bed with me every night, but at least I get to experience a variety of lovers.

~oOo~

It's Like Having
Two Husbands

When we got married, my hubby's best friend was his best man. After our marriage the friend was at our place all the time, and we all did everything together... well not everything like we do now, but every time we went out or went on a trip or vacation or camping, he was with us, and we all had a fantastic time.

He was single then. He's still actually single, but has a live-in lady friend, and she is nice too. But she never seems to want to do anything. So he still hangs out with us most of the time.

One night, I passed out from partying at our house and he stayed over because he was too drunk to drive. I was out cold on the couch in my little nightie T-shirt thingy and my hubby said he caught his friend feeling up my legs while he went to get the two of them some more beers in the kitchen. My hubby didn't let on, and he stayed out of the room to see what his friend would do.

His friend apparently stripped me, licked me, and fucked me twice while he thought my husband had gone upstairs. In the morning my hubby told me about it. He also told me how it had turned him on. I realized that I liked it too.

About a week later our friend was over again and we went out drinking at the bar together. While he and I were dancing I came right out and asked him if he had enjoyed fucking me. He looked like a deer caught in the headlights. He finally admitted it, and admitted it again in front of my husband when we got back to the table.

My husband told him he knew that he had watched him playing with me as I slept. My hubby told him, "Actually, I thought it was hot. I'm glad you finally got to sample my wife's goodies."

When the three of us got back to our place, he and I were dancing to some sexy music as my hubby was watching. I felt our friend's boner in his pants. In view of our friend's earlier exploration of my body, I undid his pants and reached in, pulling out his big hard cock. I was stroking it while my hubby watched.

I said, "I can't believe that big thing was inside me and I didn't wake up." I giggled. By then he was feeling me all over, and had undone my shirt. He started to play with my tits. I told him, "You should put your big cock back inside me, so I can see what I missed."

Well that night turned into an all-nighter. He and my hubby fucked me so hard, and in every position, and I sucked both of their cocks, and they both ate me several times. It was just beautiful, and when we woke the next day they both fucked me again... on the bed, then again in the shower.

Ever since that day, he is at our place even more than before and sometimes my hubby will come home from work to find his friend fucking me on the couch. Hubby often just sits and watches us, or he will join in. Other times I will be fucking my hubby and his friend will watch us.

A few times, all three of us have gone to the beach together. Our friend and I go for walks in the woods, and I end up with him fucking me in the woods. One time he drove while my hubby and I were in the backseat, fucking. I love being intimate with both guys so openly. I can walk around naked in front of both of them, and if I get horny I just sit on one of their big hard cocks.

My hubby and I have talked about it and we have both said that if he wasn't with his girlfriend, we would have him live with us. People think it is weird when we go out, because I am either sitting on my hubby's knee, or on our friend's knee. I regularly kiss both of them all the time, and they both treat me like I am their wife.

I have gone out on dates with just one or the other too. Usually whichever one I went out with is the one who fucks me all that night. And, if the other one wakes up, he plays with me too. I love it.

~oOo~

Getting Ready to Have
Two Husbands

Hi, my name is Lisa. I am 43 years-old. Joan, I have never written to you about me or our experiences. However, I have read about you and your two "husbands." I think your life is what has helped inspire me to do what I am about to do.

All my life I have been very sexual. I can't remember a time when I wasn't. I was coerced into having sex when I was young, but to be honest, I loved the experience. I was not beaten. I actually liked that I had sex at a young age, somewhat forced. To this day I often like being tied up during sex.

My fantasy had always been to be in a military situation and be forced to sexually please men all day for days on end. Naturally, I have shared my fantasy thoughts with my husband. He has brought me to new heights, sexually, since he and I got together.

Before I met my husband, I had sex with several men. I had been married twice and even slept around with them. In between marriages, I had sex with men I worked with, and their friends but I never dated more than one guy at a time. Until I met my husband. I never thought about having a husband and regular lovers or for that matter, ever having a man who would like to, and want to, share me with other men.

Fortunately for me, my husband loves seeing me with other men because I love having sex with different men. I like the variety of sex I get with other men. I like all types of men, black, white, Mexican, Italian, you name it. And with my husband I have had the opportunity to sample all of them, with him always being there to watch.

I never told my earlier husbands about the sex I had with others. Now, my current husband is there every time I have sex with others.

Recently, I was able to get back together with my first love, the guy I fell in love with in high school. My husband had heard me talk about Tony for years and how I wanted to get with him again. Tony's family had moved and we had lost contact.

Lately, Tony contacted me through Facebook and we got together. It was magical. When Tony and I saw each other after so many years of being apart, the electricity between us was still there. I got juicy, and he immediately got hard.

During our high school years, we had always been sexual with each other. I remember the first time I saw him in school. I told my girl friend that I would have him, and I did, that night. We had sex the night we met, and it was the best sex I have ever had. I am very much in love with my current husband, but I have to say that since Tony has come back into my life again, it is he who truly fulfills me sexually.

Of course, I have had sex with countless guys, and have enjoyed the sex I had with them, but none of them were ever like Tony. When Tony kisses me, I melt. And when we have sex it is heaven, truly. The other night I introduced my husband to Tony. They shared me. My husband is not bi-sexual, but he does love to see other men's cocks playing within me. They both played with me, but my husband let Tony take the lead.

My husband is submissive in many ways, but the other night his submissiveness gave me a feeling of having even more freedom than I already had. I was able to sit on my husband's face and let him eat me as I sucked Tony to hardness. As Tony face-fucked me, I was able to enjoy my husband licking me. I was getting the best of everything.

The three of us got together many times after that first night. Eventually my husband asked me if I would like to have Tony move in with us. I was thrilled at the idea. It was my husband who finally told Tony that we wanted him to move in with us.

Tony is moving in with us at the end of this month... and I can't wait. My husband and I have talked about this at length. My husband knows that Tony has held a big place in my heart since the day he and I met. He also knows that when Tony moves in that Tony will be my number one sex partner, not that I will limit my husband. It really can't be helped. I don't want to leave or lose my husband but I also do not want to ever lose Tony again either.

When my husband and I have talked about the three of us living together, he has said that he is okay taking a sexual back seat to Tony. I really appreciate that. It actually makes me love my husband more, for being willing to allow Tony to take his place as my primary lover while remaining my husband.

I have spoken with Tony privately and he has told me that he is willing to be my second "husband," although he and I will not be married, and he will not have the financial responsibilities of being my husband. He has also agreed to love me and have sex with me as my husband watches and/or shares in giving me pleasure. And I really do like that.

Tony will be living with us and sharing my bed with me much of the time. I am sure that many people will say that it is wrong for me to put another man ahead of my own husband, but these same people do not understand the love that Tony and I feel for each other. They also do not know how understanding and loving my husband is.

From the beginning, my husband has allowed me to have sex with others regularly since we got together. He has allowed me to get gang-banged numerous times, and to have regulars over to our home on a consistent basis.

The only difference between what we have had and now with Tony moving in with us, and instead of my husband sharing me with other men, Tony will be sharing me with my husband and with other men.

I have talked to Tony about me having sex with other men. When we were younger he shared me with a lot of his friends. So, I am sure that will not change.

When Tony moves in I will be both his wife, and my husband's wife... sort of like your situation, Joan. I will still be married to my husband, but Tony will be my number one sex partner. For the most part Tony will be able to decide who I have sex with. My husband will be in charge of all financial matters for our little "family." Tony is very dominant, whereas my husband is very submissive, like I am. Tony is very forceful sexually, which is what has always turned me on about him. Sexually he is the best I have ever had, and that is saying a lot.

I have spoken with my husband about what his role will be when Tony moves in. He and I have agreed that nothing financially will change between us, and our love for each other will not change. He understands that he will be my husband in the eyes of others, but Tony will have many of the perks of being my husband.

I feel like the luckiest woman in the world and I love my husband more than I ever have. Being shared, whether you are the wife or the husband, is the best part of marriage as far as I am concerned.

~oOo~

Her Report On
Their Large Poly Family

I thought you would enjoy learning about our large poly family here in Ohio.

I have a husband and two lovers who have lived with us for some time now. Then our family began to grow.

We recently had to move to a much bigger house because me, my husband, my two lovers, my husband's girlfriend, his ex-wife, her girlfriend, our friends and their sons, my sister and her lover, my husband's ex-wife's sister and her husband and a friend's niece, my brother and his friend, and one of my lover's friends… all live together.

So on the female side there is me, my husband's ex, her girlfriend, my sister, my husband's ex-wife's sister, my husband's girlfriend, our friend's wife (who can't have physical sex other than oral) and our friend's niece.

In other words, my husband and the other guys have lots of pussy to choose from.

For me? There is my husband and my two lovers (whom I consider to be my husbands too), our friend's husband and his sons, my brother and his friend, the two brother-in-laws, and another of my lovers (recently joined us), all in one house.

That is seven women and eleven men who enjoy having sex with each other. We all have a variety to choose from in our new house. We shared before, but now it is so much more convenient.

I do love having so many men to have sex with. And I think the men deserve the variety as much as we women do. I wouldn't want it any other way.

The End

Here is a sample from another story you may enjoy:

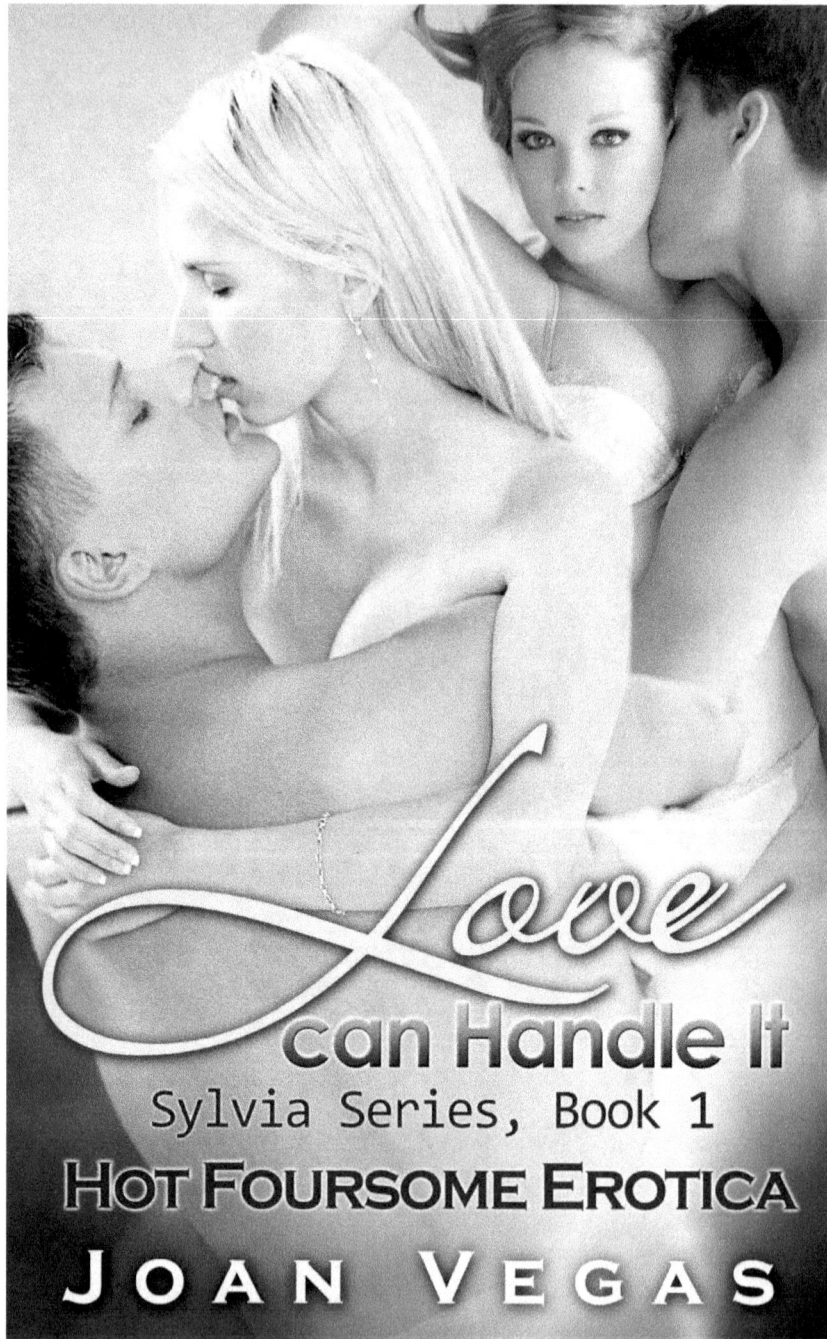

Love

can Handle It

Sylvia Series, Book 1

HOT FOURSOME EROTICA

JOAN VEGAS

Dear Joan,

I don't know why I'm doing this. My husband (Bruno) insists that I write you about my expressed resistance to three-way sex.

Would I like a three-way? Actually, yes... I think. Even after thirteen years of marriage, Bruno apparently doesn't know how much I really love to fuck. Bruno makes me cum, and many times he gives me multiple orgasms. But to be honest, I'm never quite as satisfied as I would like to be. So, I think having another man in out bed "to supplement" his love-making could be very good for me.

I'm going to be very candid with you. I'm scared to death of what might come of this. Suppose I develop romantic feelings for this other partner? Suppose he satisfies me better than Bruno? Suppose all I want is this new partner?

-Sylvia

* * *

Dear Sylvia,

You sound like the perfect female candidate to enjoy MFM three-way fun. First, you indicate that Bruno gives you lots of pleasure. Second, you indicate that you like to "fuck," and are "never quite as satisfied as (you) would like to be." Third, you obviously have a husband who is encouraging you to try one or more threesome experiences.

Apparently, the only hang-up is your fear that you may end up developing romantic feelings for the extra guy more than you love Bruno. Believe me, if you really love Bruno now... an MFM experience will not change that.

Sure, some other guy MAY give you more of certain kinds of sexual satisfaction than Bruno does. More likely, the experience of having two guys give you pleasure is the thing that is likely to give you more sexual satisfaction than you get from one guy (Bruno) alone. That is a good problem! Keep in mind that that experience is one provided for you BY Bruno... and he therefore gets all the credit for that special pleasure that you will be experiencing.

The "never quite as satisfied" part is what really leads me to believe you and Bruno are perfect candidates for some great MFM experiences. Frankly, most guys (in a one-on-one situation) can't begin to give sensual women (such as us) all the pleasure that we would like. For that reason, many sensual women begin to have affairs, etc. in an attempt to "scratch that extra itch". MFM threesomes... set up by the husband, and with his blessing... are a much more wholesome way to "scratch that extra itch" and provide new levels of feminine fulfillment for us.

Write me more about your "feelings." That seemed to be what you were about to talk about. Tell me your other thoughts and questions too. Tell me how Bruno hoped to set up an MFM experience for you.

I await hearing more from you.

Much love,
Joan

* * *

Dear Joan,

Thanks for responding to me.

The things you told me are in many ways the things Bruno told me too, i.e. great sexual satisfaction for me. Although I lied and told him he was all the satisfaction I needed. But it's not true, and I think he knows it.

You asked how he wanted to set it up. I don't know. I wouldn't let him get that far. And I have no idea with whom, although I do know a couple of men who I'm sure would volunteer.

Do I dare?

-*Sylvia*

* * *

Dear Sylvia,

As I said earlier, in my opinion virtually no one man is really "enough" for a truly sensual woman. And, it certainly is no sin to be a sensual woman! So, if Bruno "knows" that your comment (that he is "enough" for you) may be less than accurate... all the better. It just helps make things easier for the two of you to move toward the SHARED FUN of MFM pleasure.

For some reason, God created woman with a sexual capacity that typically extends far beyond what one man can comfortably satisfy. Men seem to have intense, brief sexual capacity... that, when augmented by another guy can allow a woman to experience sexual fulfillment at much higher levels. Then, man number one can watch and enjoy the woman's pleasure as he rests, before returning to the action to add another round of pleasure for that receptive, sensual woman.

Also, when we women are in our twenties, we typically are less interested in exploring new sensual things (I wasn't, but I'm not typical). Then our desire for sexual fulfillment tends to grow as we go through our later twenties, our thirties and forties. But men tend to have very high libidos from their late teens on... and their capacity for extended sex play often tends to dwindle as the years go by. Strange, how that works out. But, because of that, that's why many couples opt for exploring MFM fun.

It sounds like Bruno would like you to join him in exploring MFM fun... and it sounds like (down deep) you know this could lead to some highly erotic experiences FOR BOTH OF YOU!

The men and women in too many couples choose to scratch their sexual curiosity itch through affairs. While those who choose that route often have great momentary pleasure, they are often plagued by self-doubt and guilt afterword... and they risk upsetting their marriages and all the good things associated with their primary relationships.

When couples (such as you and Bruno could do) choose to simply "Say Yes" to giving threesomes a try, they can begin moving their SHARED sensuality to a new, higher level... one that involves both parties in inviting extra people into their sex lives... and one that assures that each party feels that they are intimately involved in the special pleasures the other gets to enjoy. When a couple JOINTLY decides to give threesomes a try, the husband usually feels that HER extra pleasure is happening because HE made it happen. It is HIS GIFT TO HER.

Occasionally, couples that first try some MFM experiences will then try exploring a few FMF experiences... where he gets to be the center of sexual attention... and that can be HER GIFT TO HIM. Even when couples stick with or return to more HER-centered threesome fun, the husband typically is comfortable with the wife being the center-piece (no pun intended) of the sexual adventures.

I can't tell you how many men have written to me to tell me how they thoroughly enjoy watching their wife as she is being pleasured by another guy... or holding her as another guy nibbles on or fills her pussy with a "strange" cock. Men tell me they enjoy letting their cock slide through their wife's pussy after another guy's cock has warmed (and maybe lubed) it. I know my two guys enjoy that... and who am I to question why?

Sylvia... I think it is time that you finally said, "OK Bruno, if you want me to try a threesome... then I will... but only if you are sure that is what YOU want. And, if it ever really happens, I want you to hold me in your arms and neck with me while it happens... so I can feel that such an experience is simply an extension of OUR shared sexual pleasure."

If you can say that (or something similar) to Bruno, I am sure he will go wild as he begins thinking about how to make it happen. After the above conversation would be the time to ask him how he thinks he could make such an experience happen. If you are comfortable with making suggestions, you could mention any of the men you know who you think you would enjoy... and who you think might be receptive.

However, an important consideration is this: Let Bruno be MOSTLY in charge of setting things up. AND, make sure that you focus your attention on Bruno (to the extent that you can) during that first half dozen or so experiences... and repeatedly re-express your love for him... and thank him for making those pleasure experiences possible. Then... ENJOY YOURSELF!!!

You ended your last note with "Do I dare?" Yes Sylvia... you most definitely should "dare"... to advance your own levels of pleasure, and to cement a new and expanded bond between you and Bruno. Let him know that your pussy is his... and if he wants it to be explored by new and different cocks... you will no longer say no. Let him know that your breasts are his breasts... and if he wants to allow other mouths and hands to caress them... you are willing to cooperate, and see what new SHARED pleasures may result.

Sylvia... I can assure you... from personal experience... that when a woman allows herself the luxury of new-guy or multiple-guy sexual stimulation... her feminine fulfillment level will reach new heights. And, when her husband makes it all possible, it truly is a gift from HIM... for their shared enjoyment.

Keep me posted.

Much love,
Joan

* * *

Dear Joan,

Thank you for the very nice and obviously very sincere note. You have given me a feeling of relaxation over this.

I'm having a real problem with the "who" in this arrangement. We have a couple of friends, married friends, who have come on to me over the years, and to whom I'm attracted. Are they out of bounds? From some of the things they have said to us, I think they may be swingers. I don't know if Bruno could bring someone that close into our sex lives.

I almost raped Bruno last night. He knows I'm turning-on to his threesome suggestions. He started talking about a threesome as he was fucking me, unfairly in the middle of my first orgasm. I'm afraid I tacitly agreed. By the way, as a lover he can last a long time. And he's big. I just wish he were enough.

-Sylvia

If you enjoyed this sample then look for **Love Can Handle It.**

Also by this Author:

Nine Guys Share Their Wives

Sharing Husbands

A Game for Three

18 Guys on Being the Extra Guy

Aussie Wife gets Naughty

Wife Enjoys Pleasure of MFM

Our Studly Neighbor

A Taste of MFM

The Stinging Nettle

Wife Sharing Fiesta

Caught in the Midst of Two

Sandwiched by Two

About the Author

Joan Vegas was born in 1973 and grew up in a small town in mid-USA.

After graduating from college, she met two guys. Both were really special and she fell in love with both of them. She was fortunate that they love her so much. They then decided to "share" her. The three of them moved in together, later on forming a "family partnership". They eventually had four children together (the story behind it is very interesting).

Because of their unique three-way partnership family, she has gotten to know other couples where a third person was regularly a part of their intimate relationships. It is the correspondence to/from these other advocates of three-way intimacy relationships that Joan's true reports are based on. And yes, it can happen... It can be very fun, intimate, and wonderful!

"Thank you for reading my stories/reports. If you are part of a three-way intimate relationship, I would love to hear from you." -Joan-

From the Author

Check my page on Amazon and my blog for Updates and interesting info.

Author Central Page - http://amzn.to/14ZEmfs
Author Blog - http://joan-vegas.awesomeauthors.org/

If you enjoyed any of my books then please share the love and click like on my books in Amazon.

If you write me a review and send me an email I will send you a free book, or many.
(Just know that these emails are filtered by my publisher.)

Good news is always welcome.

One Last Thing, For Kindle Readers...

When you turn the page, Kindle will give you the opportunity to rate this book and share your thoughts on Facebook and Twitter. If you enjoyed my writings, would you please take a few seconds to let your friends know about it? Because... when they enjoy they will be grateful to you and so will I.

Thank You!

Joan Vegas
joan_vegas@awesomeauthors.org